This Walker book belongs to:

✷ ✷ ✷ ✷ ✷ ✷ ✷ ✷ ✷ ✷ ✷ ✷ ✷ ✷ ✷ ✷ ✷ ✷ ✷ ✷

✷ ✷ ✷ ✷ ✷ ✷ ✷ ✷ ✷ ✷ ✷ ✷ ✷ ✷ ✷ ✷ ✷ ✷ ✷ ✷

For Emma, Elsie and Emile… M.R.
For Frazer McGown love Aunty Gilly

First published 2015 by Walker Books Ltd, 87 Vauxhall Walk, London SE11 5HJ
This edition published 2016 for Scottish Book Trust
Text © 2015 Michael Rosen
Illustrations © 2015 Gillian Tyler
The right of Michael Rosen and Gillian Tyler to be identified as author and illustrator respectively of this work
has been asserted by them in accordance with the Copyright Designs and Patents Act 1988
This book has been typeset in AT Arta
Printed in China
British Library Cataloguing in Publication Data:
a catalogue record for this book is available from the British Library
ISBN 978-1-4063-7618-0
10 9 8 7 6 5 4 3 2 1
www.walker.co.uk

The Bus Is For Us

Michael Rosen

Gillian Tyler

WALKER BOOKS
AND SUBSIDIARIES

LONDON • BOSTON • SYDNEY • AUCKLAND

I really like
to ride my bike

I like going far
in our car

YR2APY

When it

starts to rain

I like

the train.

BUS4US

But best is the bus.
The bus is for us.

I do of course

like riding a horse

I like to float
in a little boat

I like trips
in big ships.

But best is the bus.

**The bus
is for us.**

Sometimes I wish
I could ride on a fish

If I was allowed

I'd sit on a cloud

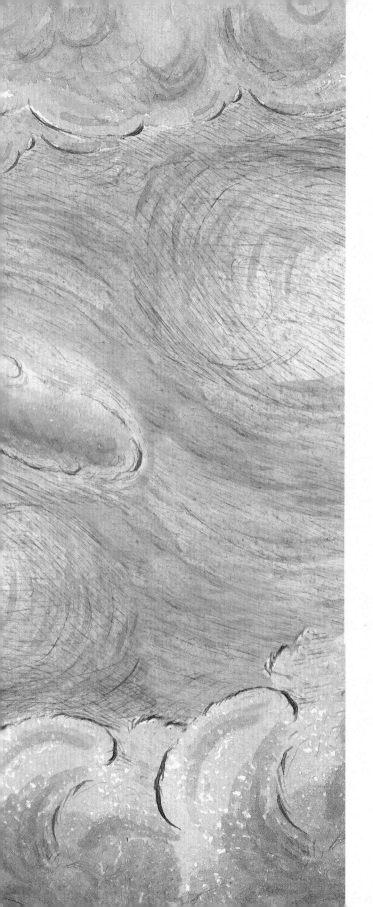

I'd be all right
up high on a kite.

But best is the bus.
The bus is for us.

I'd love to play

in an open sleigh

Fly to the moon
in a hot-air balloon

Or for a dare
ride on a bear.

But even so

the bus is best.

Best is the bus.

That's because

**the bus
is for US!**